Sometimes You Need a

jellyfish

Words & Pictures by Christopher Routly

Published by

Wasabi Books, LLC., Portland, OR
Written and Illustrated by Christopher Routly

ISBN: 978-0-9863231-0-2
10 9 8 7 6 5 4 3 2 1

Send questions, comments, or feedback to chris@jellyfishbook.com

Books available for purchase at **www.jellyfishbook.com**. Books may also be purchased in quantity by contacting the publisher, Wasabi Books, LLC, at **inquiries@wasabibooks.com**.

Printed in PRC

For Tucker and Coltrane,
my best collaborations.

Perry and Parker were
packing their packs,
to go see their
Nana and Pop.

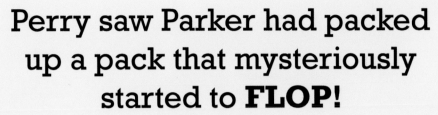

Perry saw Parker had packed
up a pack that mysteriously
started to **FLOP!**

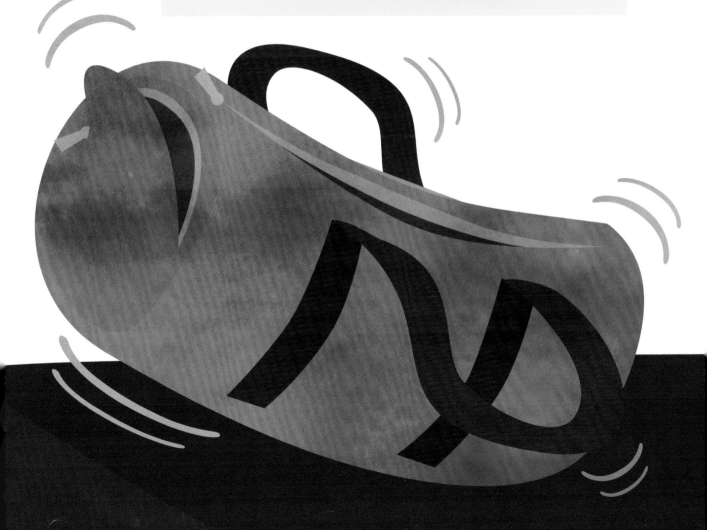

A jellyfish!

Yup.

Yep!

Now, wait just a minute!
You don't understand.

I can think
of a **ton** of good cases,
why a *jellyfish friend*,
who was closely at hand,
would be useful . . .

. . . in all **sorts** of places!

What if I needed to jump from a plane . . .

. . . and didn't have a parachute?

What if a cop needs a tentacled arm . . .

. . . to catch robbers, when hot in pursuit?

Well, I've got an instant umbrella!

And if my duet partner loses his **voice?**

Jellyfish sing **superb** *a cappella!*

I've **even** heard jellyfish
can lend a tentacle
helping to clean up your room.

Need a few extra, to help you move house?
Just invite a *whole jellyfish bloom!*

If you were a zookeeper, what better help...

Scared of the dark?

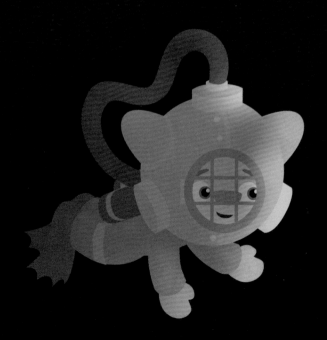

One kind of jellyfish
bioluminescently glows!

I **once**
knew a guy
who used
jellyfish pillows
to sleep
every night
in his bed.

Zzz...

Zzz...

And, **obviously**, a *jellyfish hat* would look **fabulous** up on my head!

And he turned to **his** pack with a **laugh.**

Ha ha!

And why **sometimes** you need . . .

to be continued in...
Sometimes You Need a
GIRAFFE

A cappella - Singing that is not accompanied by instruments.

Bioluminescence - Combining "bios" (Greek for "living") and "lumen" (Latin for "light"), bioluminescence is what we call it when living creatures produce light naturally, under certain conditions. At least one jellyfish has the ability, *Aequorea victoria*, also called the "crystal jelly."

Bloom - A large group, or "swarm," of jellyfish, that can number in the hundreds, or even thousands! They are formed when ocean currents move jellyfish into an area rich in nutrients and low in natural predators.

Coherent - When speaking of a person, this refers to their ability to speak clearly and logically. (Jellyfish, of course, can't speak at all.)

Inherent - A permanent and unchanging quality or attribute. Despite some of the silliness in this book, real jellyfish are *inherent* to life in watery environments only, such as oceans and lakes.

Kelp - A variety of large seaweed that is known for growing in vast "forests" in the ocean. Kelp can grow as quickly as a foot and a half a day, to heights of over 250 feet!

thank you!

This book would not exist without the support and generosity of the following wonderful, wise, witty (and I hear also very attractive) people:

Robert (Jay) Wisniewski • The Schmelzenbach Family • Mike • Julie Pugh • Jeff Bogle • Anonymous • Owen & Layla Jacobs • Saint Pillsbury • LisaCaitlin Hess • Charlotte • Lindsay Bryant • Jess & Thijs • Beatrice Reback • Jeff Tepper • David Jaggie • Larry Interrante • Homesweet Homegrown • Bridget & Leo Johnson • Matt Peregoy • Joel E. Martin • Desiree Kern • Zeb Hannon • Derek W • Loretta Green • Beki Bergeron • Kai, Brian, & Kay Widmer • Kristen Radic • Amateur Idiot•Professional Dad • Oren, Talia, & Sivan • Justin Faucette • Chardonae & Brielyn Manuel • Michael Griffin • James Hudyma • Michael Moebes • Carter & Gavin Zelenka • Danielle, Dom & Sol Black Lyons • Holly Higgins • Tyler, Carey, & Elijah • Christine Stewart • Mark Monlux • Brent Almond • The Blackman Boyz • Frida & Lewis • Nicki Reimert • George Spillett • Gray Family • Daniel De Guia • Lucia • R.C., Kelley, & Avery Liley • Hattie, Tilly, & Jasper Miller • Jim Altstatt • Scott Erickson • Phil Corless • James G. Kline • Natalie Stewart • Emil Rutkowski • Will Culp • Luke Spector • Trey & Cody Johnson • D.J. & Ashley Cole • Shraddha Aryal • Chris Brown • The Butterworth Fam • Genevieve Johann • Chris Masek • Tiphanie B. • Dee Wirick Davis • Nick Browne - papabrownie.com • Jensen, Quinn & Carson Neal • @DaDaRocks • Dowling family • Karen Mendez • Sofia & Aiden Aragon • McPherson Family • Jim & Sandie Merrifield • Christopher Persley • Jeff Walters • Owen & Dylan Major • Tom Burns • Jesse James Boulton • Sam Christensen • Rian & Caleb Brandy • Mylene Sararas •

Logan Wallace • Aron & Shari Dick • Alex Harwood • W. Elizabeth Chapin • Jeff Hay • Kasper Breisnes • Anonymous • Andrew • Mac Cherry • Jimmy, Irene & Amelia • Annie Bethancourt • Christopher VanDijk • Scarlet Maxfield • Patrick, Lisa & James Cannon • Eric, Jess & Harrison Covell • Jay, Shana, Beckett & Cooper Sokol • Rebekah Kamer • Charlie & Zacharie • Oren • Wesley Family • Donna Wade • Charlie Seymour Jr • The Tavill Family • Jill Noble • The Curry Family • Kristopher Jansma • Karen Keltz • Ken, Anna & Julia Levin • Lisa Humerickhouse • Henry Elliss • Christy Leonard • Clay Nichols • Lily • Euan • Hannah the Glavor • Alex Coates for Gareth & Cordy • Marc & Carolyn Scaife • Lydia • J. Parrish Lewis • The Lewis Family • Kennedy & Jefferson Fowler • Audra Pace • Ryan E. Hamilton • Tito Aman • Jacob & Charlie Casson • Aimee Driskill • Dave, Maia, Bren, Jace, Joel, Bryce, Seth & Zane Routly • Vibe of Portland • Ian, Melissa, Morgan & Elliott Brown • Lee & Gaila Palo • Colleen Coyne & Bart Brinkman • Dan & Carrie Potter • Valerie Guay • Kirk Holloway

special thanks to

Grace Vitrano • Christi & Jason Olson • The Cartera • Jonathan Petersen • Shawn & Ken Stansbury • Ryan Rippentrop Family • Jay Garrison & Erin Stephenson • Chris, Susie, Adam, Sarah & Heidi Bernholdt • Dave Hershey • Lucy & Emi Sperber • Carl Wilke • Cornelius Wilke • George & Jo Ann Widmer • Ishwaria & Vivek Subbiah • Spencer Yonker • Roffel Family • Luke & Erin Cummings • Robert Burnell • The Tamura Family • Doug & John • Paul Gilbride • Adam & Owen Grasso • The Schneider Family • Phil & Elsie Routly • Mark & Pamela Widmer

...and of course my lovely and amazing wife Anna, the best partner a guy could ever want.

also available by christopher routly

The Animal **alphabet**
Words & Pictures by Christopher Routly

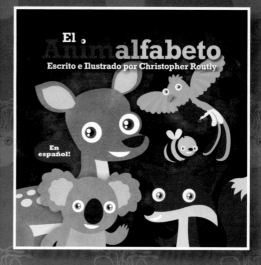

El Animal**alfabeto**
Escrito e Ilustrado por Christopher Routly

En español!

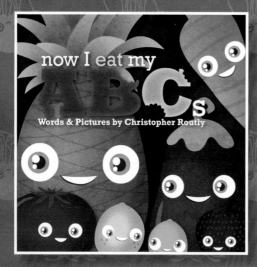

now I eat my **ABCs**
Words & Pictures by Christopher Routly

SketchBoy
LIFE OF **RONNIE**
BY CHRISTOPHER ROUTLY

VOLUME 1:
MAKING IT UP
AS I GO ALONG